WHERE BEAR?

by
Sophy Henn

PHILOMEL BOOKS

An Imprint of Penguin Group (USA)

Once there was a
bear cub . . .

who lived with
a little boy.

But over time the bear cub grew . . .

and grew . . .

AND GREW!

And did things
that bears do . . .

and do . . .

One day, the boy looked at the bear and realized
he was just too big and bearish to be living
in a house.

"I think it's time we found you a new place to live
where you can be bearish and big,"
said the boy. "But where, bear?"

"There are bears in the toy shop,"
said the boy. "The toy shop is great."

"NO,"
said the bear.

"Then where, bear?" asked the boy.

"Oh, hang on!
There are bears at the zoo!"
said the boy.
"What about the zoo?"

"NO,"
said the bear.

"Then where, bear?"
asked the boy.

"I've seen bears at the circus,"
said the boy. "What about the circus?"

"I know,
bears live in the woods,"
said the boy.
"What about the
woods, bear?"

"NO,"
said the bear.

"Then where, bear?"
asked the boy.

"Lots of bears live in caves,"
said the boy.
"Would you like
to live in a cave?"

"I think bears
live in the jungle,"
said the boy.
"What do you think, bear?"

"NO,"
whispered
the bear.

"Then where, bear?" asked the boy.

"Hmmm,"
    said the boy.

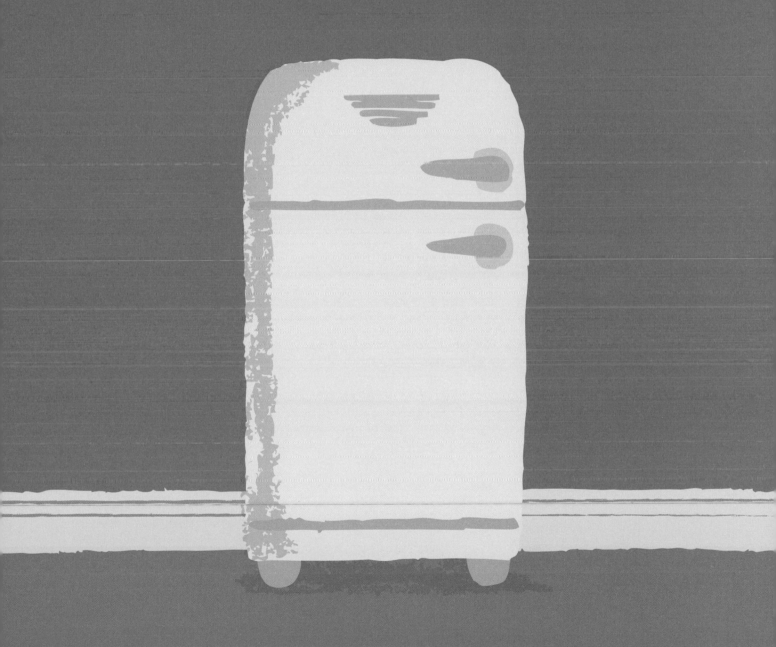

The bear said nothing.

"I'VE GOT IT!"
said the boy.
"Some bears live in the Arctic.
What about it, bear?"

"SNOW,"
said the bear.

"There,"
said the boy.

And the boy went home.

So the bear was happy.

And the boy was happy.

And they stayed the
very best of friends . . .

. . . chit-chattering
on the phone
all the time.

"We should go somewhere together
like we used to,"
said the bear.

"But where, bear?"
asked the boy.

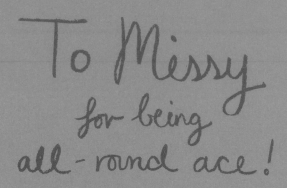

To Missy
for being
all - round ace!

PHILOMEL BOOKS
Published by the Penguin Group | Penguin Group (USA) LLC
375 Hudson Street, New York, NY 10014

USA | Canada | UK | Ireland | Australia | New Zealand | India | South Africa | China
penguin.com | A Penguin Random House Company

Copyright © 2015 by Sophy Henn.
First American edition published in 2015 by Philomel Books. Published in Great Britain by Penguin Group (UK) in 2015.
Penguin supports copyright. Copyright fuels creativity, encourages diverse voices, promotes free speech, and creates a vibrant
culture. Thank you for buying an authorized edition of this book and for complying with copyright laws by not reproducing,
scanning, or distributing any part of it in any form without permission. You are supporting writers and allowing Penguin to
continue to publish books for every reader.

Library of Congress Cataloging-in-Publication Data is available upon request.
Manufactured in China by South China Printing Co. Ltd. | Text set in Clarendon Cn BT Bold. | ISBN 978-0-399-17158-1
1 3 5 7 9 10 8 6 4 2